ARMADILLO AND HARE
AND THE
VERY NOISY BEAR

www.davidficklingbooks.com

Small Tales from the Big Forest

Armadillo and Hare

JEREMY STRONG
SMALL TALES FROM THE BIG FOREST
ARMADILLO AND HARE
AND THE
VERY NOISY BEAR

ILLUSTRATED BY REBECCA BAGLEY

David Fickling Books

31 Beaumont Street
Oxford OX1 2NP, UK

Armadillo and Hare and the Very Noisy Bear
is a
DAVID FICKLING BOOK

First published in Great Britain in 2020 by
David Fickling Books,
31 Beaumont Street,
Oxford, OX1 2NP

Text © Jeremy Strong, 2020
Illustrations © Rebecca Bagley, 2020

978-1-78845-106-2

1 3 5 7 9 10 8 6 4 2

Papers used by David Fickling Books are from well-
managed forests and other responsible sources.

MIX
Paper from
responsible sources
FSC® C018072

DAVID FICKLING BOOKS Reg. No. 8340307

A CIP catalogue record for this book is available from the British Library.

Printed and bound in Great Britain by Clays Ltd, Elcograf S.p.A.

For all the small animals in my life, especially Joe, Noah, Niamh and Freya. JS

For all the little animals in this Big Forest, but especially mine in our Little one. RB

Contents

A Celebration

It was a warm and sunny morning. Only two small white cotton-wool clouds could be seen floating in the endless blue of the sky. Birds flickered amongst the trees singing greetings to the world of the Big Forest.

Armadillo was shuffling about in his dressing gown and his old comfy red slippers. He had dragged a table on to the front porch for breakfast. He laid a blue and white chequered table cloth over the top. There were two blue place mats and two blue napkins. Armadillo's second favourite colour was blue. (His first was cheese-colour.)

There was also a bowl of muesli for Hare and a lump of Gorgonzola for Armadillo.

He stood back and admired his work. Breakfast on the porch. Sunshine. Birds singing. Cheese on the table. Splendid!

Hare came outside in his blue pyjamas, the ones with little stars on them. He beamed when he saw the breakfast table.

'You have been busy!' Hare exclaimed. 'There's my muesli! Thank you, Armadillo. Oh, I see you've got your stinky cheese.' Hare's nose and whiskers wrinkled.

'Hare, you know very well that this is my "wake-up" cheese. It has such a tang on the tongue, it makes my brain whirr and whizz like an electricity power station.'

They sat down at the little table and began

to eat. Every so often one of them would lean back in his chair and gaze out at the flower-dotted meadow.

Hare gave a happy sigh. 'Such a beautiful day,' he murmured. His eyes closed and his extraordinary ears began to softly stroke each other. Hare's ears always did that when he was thinking – or dreaming.

Now he opened his eyes, looked at his old friend across the table, and smiled. 'I was remembering how we met,' he said.

Armadillo chuckled. 'It wasn't a day like this!'

'No it wasn't,' Hare agreed. 'The rain! The thunder and lightning! You know I can't stand storms. I was terrified.'

'You were also very, very wet,' Armadillo reminded him. 'There was a loud banging on the door, and when I opened it there you were, looking like a wet dishcloth, with ears. I don't think I have ever seen such a bedraggled mess of an animal before or since.'

Hare smiled again. 'But you

took me in and I stood by your fire and made a huge wet puddle on the floor. You could have sent me away. But you didn't.'

Armadillo frowned. 'Well, I wouldn't have wanted any creature to be out in such a dreadful storm.' He reached for a bit of bread and carefully spread it with more Gorgonzola. 'Besides,' he added mischievously, 'I had no idea how much trouble you would be.'

Hare's ears gave a cheerful flick. 'Nonsense. I was the perfect guest and you, dear Armadillo, were lonely.'

'Lonely? Me? I like my own company.'

'You were lonely,' Hare repeated.

'Only a tiny bit.'

'Big enough of a bit to let me stay,' Hare pointed out, chewing the last spoonful of muesli.

'Oh, psshhh!' Armadillo pulled a grouchy face. It made Hare laugh so hard half the muesli splattered from his mouth.

'See what I mean? You're nothing but trouble.' Armadillo's shoulders heaved with silent laughter while he took his napkin and brushed off the bits of muesli stuck to the front of his dressing gown.

He went on. 'Do you realise, Hare, it's exactly one year, five months and twenty-three and a half days since you arrived on my doorstep? I think we should celebrate, a party maybe.'

'A party!' breathed Hare. If anyone liked parties, it was Hare. His ears made frantic signals in every direction, and his whiskers positively danced.

Everyone was invited. Wombat arrived on her bicycle, with a lot of parping and pinging. Tortoise and Lobster were sitting in the little basket that hung over the handlebars.

'Otherwise they might never have got here in time,' said Wombat, winking at Hare.

Lobster shuffled indignantly into the cabin.

'Actually I can move pretty fast,' she snapped.

Elephant and Jaguar came out of the Big Forest. Invisible Stick Insect hitched a ride on Jaguar's head, sitting between her ears. Nobody noticed of course. She was invisible, after all.

Giraffe strode across the meadow to the cabin door and wanted to know what kind of party it was going to be.

'It's a sitting-down party, Giraffe,' Armadillo declared. 'It's not a standing up party. If you

stand up your head will go through the ceiling
and if Elephant stands up he'll probably break
everything. I think you and Elephant go by
the window and we will pass cakes out to you.
I wouldn't want you to miss out and we can
still chat.'

But just as everyone managed to squeeze
into the little cabin, all the lights went out.
Blackness filled every corner. A chorus of
startled voices sang out.

'What's happened?'

'Why is it dark?'

'Ow! Someone trod on my foot.'

'Is that a wardrobe I'm bumping into or is it Elephant?'

Armadillo tried to calm everyone. 'Be patient. I'll find a candle. The electricity has gone off.'

There was only one candle, and it gave off a rather faint light.

'We can't have a party in the dark,' Tortoise announced. 'Parties need lots of light.'

Wombat made her way carefully across to Armadillo. She told him that if he brought the candle she could check the electric wiring upstairs in the attic. Wombat was an excellent electrician, plumber and general handywoman,

not to mention her acrobatics on her bicycle.
'It's probably a loose wire,' she told him.

'If we take the candle it will be completely
dark down here,' Armadillo pointed out.

Jaguar smiled, showing her glinting teeth.
'I like the dark,' she purred ominously.

'I think I might be able to help there,'
suggested Hare brightly. 'I can play my tuba
and hopefully something party-ish will float
out of the top.'

So he did, and tried very hard to play light
music. Out of the top of the tuba
came fireflies and glow-worms,
tiny dancing fireworks and
bright neon signs that said
'CAFÉ', 'DOUGHNUTS'
and 'CAR WASH'. (Hare

had no idea about that last one.) They drifted over the heads of the animals and slowly vanished, only to be replaced by more as Hare played on.

Meanwhile, upstairs, Wombat was crawling amongst the wiring while Armadillo held the candle for her. She was trying to find where the wiring was broken. It did not take her long because she could now hear an angry, electric buzzing noise. There, beside two ends of a broken

wire, Wombat found a small, very fuzzy and scared mouse. Her jagged tail was sticking straight up into the air like frozen lightning. It was clear that Mouse had chewed through the cable and the electric shock had made her tail turn into a lightning bolt and her body into a hair brush.

Mouse's body was still fizzing with electricity. Armadillo and Wombat both noticed that she seemed to be rather elderly. Mouse was leaning on a small walking stick and it reminded Armadillo of his own mother.

When she was old she had needed a mobility scooter. Armadillo sighed.

'Mouse,' he began, rather gruffly. 'I hope you're all right, but you have plunged my house into darkness just as we were having a party downstairs.'

Mouse was still trembling and her voice was unsteady. 'Such a shock. Urgh! I was hungry. No food for days. I–I was sure I'd find something in your attic. I'm so sorry I've ruined your party.' Mouse's eyes brimmed with tears.

Wombat looked at Armadillo and raised one bushy eyebrow. What was Armadillo to do?

Armadillo's shoulders heaved a sigh. 'Hmm. Wombat, can you repair the wiring?'

'Of course. It's my job. I'm switching off

the electricity supply here. I'm putting these two ends back together. Then I'm switching it back on and – there!'

Suddenly the house was filled with light. A cheer rose up the stairs from below.

'Thank you, Wombat,' said Armadillo. 'Now then, Mouse, you pop into my cardigan pocket. We are going downstairs to eat. There are friends down there. Lobster, Tortoise, Jaguar—'

'Jaguar!' Mouse almost had a heart attack.

'Yes, but don't be afraid. Jaguar can be quite civilised, especially when there's cake to eat. There's always cake at parties. Anyhow, this is my house and you are safe with me.'

Nevertheless, Mouse decided she would stay in the warm comfort of Armadillo's cardigan pocket. He gave her several crumbs of his favourite Gorgonzola cheese. He told her that he would make sure he left more crumbs out at night, just for her.

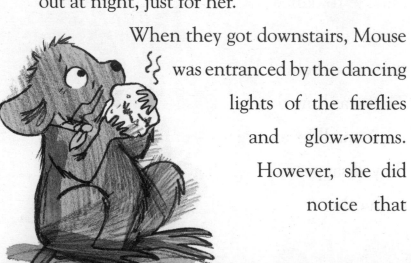

When they got downstairs, Mouse was entranced by the dancing lights of the fireflies and glow-worms. However, she did notice that

Jaguar kept
looking at her
in a fond kind
of way. Mouse
thought it
might have been
a friendly kind of fondness but she wasn't
sure. She ducked back down into the safety of
Armadillo's cardigan pocket.

The party was a great success. They all went
outside to dance, while Hare played his tuba.
Then all the animals made a long, dancing
line, one behind the other, led by Giraffe.
That was how they made their way home,

Armadillo and Hare watched them until
they disappeared from sight. They smiled at
each other.

'Time for bed,' said Armadillo.

'Indeed,' said Hare, putting down his tuba. 'Goodnight, Armadillo.'

'Goodnight, Hare. Goodnight, Mouse,' Armadillo added, peering into his pocket. 'Oh, she's already fast asleep.'

Armadillo tiptoed upstairs to his bedroom.

The Noise

Armadillo thought it was the most awful racket he had ever heard. The most tremendous bashing and crashing had been going on for fifteen minutes. He found one of Hare's much-loved scarves and wrapped it round his ears. It didn't make much difference.

He went out on to the porch. The noise was even louder, but the grassy meadow in front of the little log cabin was empty.

'What on earth is it?' he growled. 'Where is it coming from?'

Hare was fascinated. His long ears were

leaning towards the noise as if strong magnets were at work. 'I think it sounds quite exciting,' said Hare, his eyes big and round, staring towards the deafening, invisible clamour.

Armadillo turned his head sharply towards his friend. 'Exciting?' he repeated. 'Exciting? It sounds as if the world is coming to an end.'

Hare gave Armadillo a challenging look. 'It's called music,' he declared.

'It's called NOISE and I don't like it. If you think that's music maybe you should go and see where it's coming from and ask them to turn it down. It's giving me toothache.'

'If you ask me, it's all those sweet biscuits you like eating with your cheese that's giving you toothache,' Hare told his friend.

'Well, I didn't ask you, did I?' Armadillo

answered. 'I suppose we shall have to go and find out just what is making that – cacophony.'

'You'd better give me my scarf back if we're going out. Stick your paws in your ears instead.' Hare smiled to himself. Silly old Armadillo!

Hare soon discovered that he wasn't the only one excited by all the throbbing, bashing and crashing that was going on. There was a sudden pinging and parping and Wombat came cycling past. She was riding no-hands because she was trying to hold down a baseball cap on her head as well as operating her bicycle bell and horn. The cap was several sizes too big and kept flopping about. Nevertheless, it rather suited Wombat. Hare thought so too. With a hat like that *and* one of his famous scarves he would

look very smart indeed.

'I found it on the branch of a tree,' Wombat explained, breathless from pedalling. 'I suppose it must belong to someone. In the meantime, I'm looking after it. Are you going to find out what that noise is?'

Hare nodded and laughed. 'Armadillo here thinks it's the end of the world.'

'Well, it is quite loud,' Wombat agreed. 'Look, there's Tortoise up ahead.'

Tortoise was not the only one ahead of them. Soon they spotted Giraffe, Jaguar and Elephant.

By this time the noise was so loud it made Hare's insides wobble. They went round a large bush and there in front of them was – The Noise.

Hare's eyes almost popped out from his head. Wombat had to do a cartwheel and a handspring. Tortoise stood on tiptoe to see better and exclaimed, 'Oh my!' several times over.

In front of them was an animal that the Big Forest had never seen before. A very large, round and fabulously white bear wearing sunglasses was smashing away on a massive set of drums and cymbals.

Giraffe, who rather fancied himself as a dancer, had already begun to sway in time to Bear's furious rhythm. Now Hare's ears began to sway and jerk too. Even Tortoise could not stop his head from bobbing from one side to the other. Mouse was trying (with great difficulty) to do a waltz inside Armadillo's cardigan pocket.

Jaguar stepped out of the Big Forest and joined the growing audience. She sat down, licked a paw and smoothed back one ear.

'What is this?' she asked Armadillo with a puzzled sigh.

'Don't ask me,' grunted Armadillo. 'Hare says it's music. I say it's NOISE.'

'Hmm.' Jaguar nodded slowly. 'I am inclined to agree. I like melodies.'

'No, no,' interrupted Tortoise, still bobbing his head. 'This is beat beat beat music.'

'Maybe, but there's no need to beat beat beat one over the head with it,' Armadillo shot back.

Jaguar gave a snort of laughter, but Tortoise was annoyed. 'Just because you don't like it doesn't mean it's bad. Others might like it.'

'And they're welcome to it,' muttered Armadillo.

'Would anyone like to dance with me?' asked Giraffe loftily, swooping his head amongst the audience.

'ME!' yelled Lobster, launching herself at one of Giraffe's four ankles and clinging on.

31

Giraffe beamed with pleasure and resumed his dance.

Tortoise poked Wombat with one foot. 'Do you mind if I stand on your shoulders to get a better view?'

'Not at all.' Wombat beamed.

But no sooner had Tortoise struggled up Wombat's back than he fell off. He toppled backwards and landed upside down with a breath-snatching crash on the grass.

The music (or The Noise) stopped at once. Bear peered anxiously over his drum set.

As soon as he saw Tortoise upside down he realised that this was an emergency. He grabbed a small white box with a red cross on it and hurried towards the accident.

'Make way! Stand back, everyone! I'm

coming through. Don't worry. I'm almost a doctor. Make way!'

The animals fell back as Bear crouched over Tortoise, who was feebly waving his legs in the air.

'Now then, where does it hurt?' demanded Bear. 'Are you bruised? Anything broken? I can't see any bleeding. That's good. Can you breathe? Can you speak? Show me your eyes. Can you do this?'

Bear went cross-eyed for a few seconds. Tortoise did the same.

'Oh, that's excellent,' declared Bear. 'That means you're alive. Keep breathing, that helps even more. Now then, I'm going to bandage you.'

Tortoise finally managed to get his breath back. 'I don't need bandages,' he told Bear. 'I just need to be turned over.'

Bear shook his head. 'No, no, no. Patients always need bandages. That's what bandages are for. Keep still.'

Soon Tortoise was muffled with bandages all the way up to his head.

'There!' said Bear. 'You'll be all right now.'

'But I'm still upside down,' Tortoise told him.

'A small point,' Bear answered, a little crossly, and he turned him over.

'I can't move my legs.'

'Are they broken?' asked Bear, sounding almost hopeful.

'No. They're tied up with bandages.'

But Bear had already turned his attention to the other animals and was introducing himself. 'Hello, everyone. I'm Bear, of the polar variety. I have come to live in the Big Forest. I'm almost a doctor. Any aches or pains, coughs or whatnots, come and see me. I also play the drums. In fact, I'm a band. I call myself "The Noise".'

'How appropriate,' Armadillo couldn't help saying.

'You were brilliant!' cried Wombat, wildly

waving her paws as if she were drumming.

Bear was suitably chuffed. 'Thank you, Wombat. I see you've found my cap! The wind blew it off, and you've found it. Thank you.'

'I did wonder where it came from,' said Wombat, handing over the cap. But she couldn't hide her disappointment. She really did like it. Bear frowned. He shook his big head.

'You know, I think it's too small for me really. Why don't you keep it? I've got another one somewhere.'

'Can I? Really? Really really? Thank you! I loved your music,' Wombat gushed.

But Jaguar disagreed. 'Hmm. I prefer proper music,' she said, stroking her pearl necklace.

'With tunes.'

Bear shook his big head. 'Oh, I don't do tunes. I'm post-tune. I'm *avant-garde*.'

'I have no idea what you mean,' said Jaguar, shaking her head. 'I don't like long words.'

'It means,' began Armadillo, 'that he's noisy. All that bashing about. I stopped doing that when I was three.'

Hare sighed. 'That's where you went wrong,' he told his friend. 'You should never have stopped. It's fun. It's exciting.'

'Yes. It's so exciting I'm going home,' muttered Armadillo. And he did. Hare trailed after him. One by one the other animals left and a calm silence descended along the edge of the Big Forest. Bear and Wombat were the last to go.

A little cough got their attention.

'Do you think you could untie my legs now?' asked Tortoise politely.

The Exhibition

Armadillo had been painting pictures all day. It was something he liked to do. He would put on his painting coat and go to his studio. (This was actually a small room at the back of the house.) Sometimes, he dreamed that he might one day be known as Armadillo, Artist. Or perhaps Armadillo, Artist and Cheese Expert. Or should that be Cheese Expert and Artist? He couldn't decide which was more important.

Today, he had created two new pictures. The first was called 'Cheese – View from the Left'. The second was called 'Cheese – View

from the Right'.

'I thought I'd do one more,' Armadillo told Hare. 'From above.'

Hare wrinkled his nose. 'So that would be called "Cheese – View from Above",' he suggested, with a twinkle in his eye.

'Hmmm,' agreed Armadillo, seriously. He put his wet brushes in a pot while Hare watched.

'Have you ever thought of painting something else?' Hare asked. 'Like, um, muesli?'

'No,' Armadillo answered. 'Why would I do that?'

Hare shook his head. It didn't really matter.

'Anyway,' Armadillo went on, 'I'm thinking of having an exhibition.'

'What sort of exhibition?' asked Hare.

'An art exhibition of my paintings. It's what artists do.'

Hare was interested. 'Where would you have your exhibition?'

'Here. Then the others can come and see. We've never had an exhibition in the Big Forest before.' Armadillo was quite taken with his idea. 'I've been looking at my work and realised that I actually have quite a lot of paintings.'

'Yes, and they're all of cheese,' Hare pointed out.

'Of course they are,' grumbled Armadillo, as if they would be of anything else.

Hare frowned. 'Do you think the others will mind? I mean, sometimes it's nice to have a bit of variety.'

Armadillo stopped what he was doing. *A bit of variety?* 'Do you mean I could do a painting called "Cheese – View from Below"?' he wondered. 'That would be difficult because whatever the cheese was on would get in the way, so you wouldn't see it – unless it was made of glass. But painting glass is difficult because you can't see glass, can you? That's the whole point of glass – you're able to see through it. So in the end, the cheese would look as if it was just floating in mid-air.'

Hare's ears were slowly tying themselves into a frustrated knot. 'I think this is getting silly,' he said flatly. 'It's not what I meant at all. I meant, why not choose another subject, like muesli or a picture of our cabin?'

Armadillo shook his head. 'No, no. I think you're right about the floating cheese.'

'But I never said anything about floating cheese,' complained Hare. 'That was something you said.'

'And I think I'm right,' Armadillo agreed with himself. 'A floating cheese.' Armadillo grinned at his friend. He seized a new canvas and put it on his easel. 'I'm going to start straight away, Hare. "Cheese – View from Below". It will be quite different.'

Hare sighed and went off to practise his tuba playing. Soon, his bedroom was filled with cheeses of all sorts and three miniature cows. He had to stop. He looked out of his window instead. In the distance he could see Elephant jumping up and down. Elephant had tied a length of rope to his tail. He held the other end with his trunk and he was trying to skip. Hare sighed even harder.

Twenty-two paintings of cheese took a surprising

amount of work. Hare was very obliging and helped bang in nails to hang the pictures on. Afterwards, the pair of them went from room to room checking everything. There were paintings in every room, even the bathroom.

Hare carefully wrote out a sign for the cabin gallery.

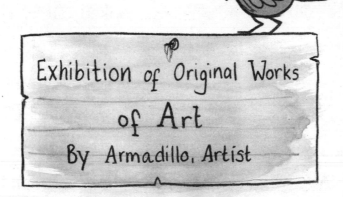

Exhibition of Original Works

of Art

By Armadillo, Artist

Armadillo had wanted Hare to add

And Cheese Expert.

but Hare managed to persuade the artist that the paintings were the important thing.

'Otherwise anyone coming to look at the paintings might expect there to be a cheese-tasting as well,' Hare said.

Armadillo clapped his paws. 'Yes! We must have nibbles, Hare. Cheese and a drink of something. There are always nibbles on the first day of an art exhibition. I read that in a magazine somewhere.'

So they put out crisps and little chunks of cheese and some biscuits.

'Not too much cheese,' grumbled Armadillo. 'Leave some for me. We're not giving them a three-course meal.'

Then the other animals began to arrive. One by one they went into each room, gazing at Armadillo's paintings. He followed them and tried to catch what they were saying about his work. He was looking forward to hearing what they thought.

Tortoise stared hard at a large painting. 'I like this one,' he told Armadillo. 'It makes me think of ancient Egypt and the pyramids.'

'Really?' Armadillo was confused. 'It's actually a wedge of cheddar.'

'It looks like a pyramid to me,' Tortoise insisted. 'With a bit knocked off the top.' Tortoise moved on to the next picture. Armadillo shook his head.

Invisible Stick Insect was delighted with a painting called 'Cheese Sandwich'. 'It's got colours that match my bedroom curtains,' she told everyone eagerly. Armadillo groaned.

Upstairs, Bear (of the polar variety) was in

the bathroom with Hare.

'I like Armadillo's sense of humour,' chuckled Bear. 'It's so funny that he's put a picture of some soap in the bathroom.'

Hare looked. Yes. Bear was sort of right. It did look like some soap, even though Hare knew it was actually cheese. Hare hoped nobody would tell Armadillo.

But the painting that caught everyone's attention was 'Cheese – View from Below'.

'Phoowee! That's a fat cloud,' said Elephant, who had finished his skipping and had come to have a look.

'The label says it's cheese.' Lobster folded her pincers across her chest.

'It IS cheese!' said Armadillo loudly. He was getting rather hot and bothered.

'In that case, it must be a floating cheese,' laughed Elephant. 'I've never seen a floating cheese.'

'It's not floating. It's on a glass table,' Armadillo growled.

'But you can't see the table,' said Lobster pointedly.

'That's because it's made of glass!'

Armadillo's whiskery snout was twitching angrily.

'And what are those four sticks doing?' Lobster pointed at them with one large claw.

'They're not sticks. Those are the table legs! Can't you tell? Are you blind? What's the matter with you all?' cried Armadillo. 'Pyramids, curtains, soap – don't you have eyes?'

Hare hurried into the room. 'Nibbles and drinks are ready outside!' he cried. 'Come on, hurry up before it all gets eaten by Elephant.'

The animals dutifully filed outside and nibbled away. One by one, they went off home, leaving Hare and Armadillo to clear up.

Armadillo did it very noisily. He kept muttering to himself about blind fools who couldn't tell a cheese from a pyramid.

Hare laid a calming paw on Armadillo's shoulder. 'You know, our friends liked your paintings.'

'But, Hare, they couldn't see!' cried Armadillo. 'They didn't understand about the

cheese and what it means, to me!'

'They liked your work,' Hare pointed out. 'So maybe they saw things in your paintings that you . . . didn't.'

Hare was silent for a few seconds. He looked around the room and pointed at an empty wall. 'Look at that wall. There's an animal face, an owl. It's an owl face. Do you see?'

Armadillo shook his head moodily. 'No, I don't.'

Hare went to the wall and pointed at some cracks. 'There's the beak. There's one eye and there's another—'

'Ah! Yes! I see it now.' Armadillo nodded. 'Those cracks make a kind of owl face.'

'But they're still cracks. There is no owl,' said Hare. 'Or can they be both at the same time?' Hare looked over the top of his glasses at his friend.

Armadillo went quiet. He was considering what Hare had said. At last he gave a small grunt. 'I still think the cheese was pretty obvious.'

Hare smiled. 'Perhaps. But listen, I have a favour to ask you, Armadillo. The new painting, the one with the floating cheese—'

'IT'S NOT FLOATING!'

'No, no. I know it's not,' Hare said hastily. 'But I like that painting. There's something mysterious and magical about it, and I would really love to have it in my bedroom.'

Armadillo looked at his friend. 'Seriously?' he asked. 'You're not just trying to please me, are you?'

'I think it's the most interesting painting you have done, and I would be honoured to hang it in my room,' Hare declared.

Armadillo rather liked the idea of one of his cheeses being mysterious and magical. He gave a nod. 'It's yours,' he told Hare. 'At least you understand the soul of an artist.'

Hare draped one arm round his friend's shoulders. 'Everyone liked your paintings,' he pointed out. 'Maybe they didn't see what you wanted them to see, but they did like them.'

Armadillo heaved a long sigh. 'I know. It's just that I wish they understood the importance of cheese.'

Swimming

Armadillo and Hare were sitting on the front porch of their little cabin. It was a warm, clear day and the bees were very busy amongst the meadow flowers. Hare was reading. Armadillo was gazing at his red slippers. He wondered how much longer they would last. He'd had them quite a while. It would be a bad day when they finally fell apart. They were the most comfy slippers he had ever had. Armadillo tried to remember previous slippers he'd worn, but a distant thumping noise was disturbing his thoughts.

He looked out across the meadow. 'What is that noise, Hare? It's going on and on. I suspect it's Bear banging those wretched drums of his.'

Hare looked up. 'It's not Bear. It's Elephant. He's practising his skipping again.'

Armadillo was astonished. 'Why on earth does Elephant want to skip?'

'I've no idea. Maybe he enjoys it. Perhaps he likes a challenge.' Hare glanced over the top of his spectacles and smiled. 'We can't all sit around admiring our slippers.'

'Or reading.' Armadillo pointed at Hare's book. 'What are you reading, anyway?'

'It's called *Thirty-Seven Ways to Wear a Scarf*. It's very interesting.'

'Sounds fascinating,' muttered Armadillo. He had no interest in scarves or any items of clothing, except how much longer his red slippers would last.

Their conversation was interrupted by the arrival of Bear (of the polar variety).

'We were just talking about you.' Armadillo sniffed and wrinkled his snout.

'I love your hat,' said Hare admiringly.

Bear seemed surprised. 'Really? It's just a hat. I don't wear it all the time.' As he spoke Bear removed his hat and studied it, as if the hat might suddenly do something extraordinary, like fly away.

'Maybe I should get a hat,' said Hare, giving Armadillo an enquiring look.

Armadillo raised his eyebrows. 'I think you might have trouble with the ears,' he pointed out. 'Where would you put them? You should think these things through, Hare.'

Bear carefully put his hat back on. 'Actually, I came to tell you that I am starting a swimming club.'

'A swimming club?' repeated Armadillo. 'Why would you do that?'

'Lots of animals can't swim, so I thought I would start a club and teach them, being pretty good at it myself.'

Armadillo looked at Hare and shrugged, as if it was the maddest idea he had ever heard. But Hare was interested.

'Yes!' he exclaimed. 'I'd love to do that. I have to say, I am not a good swimmer at all.'

'Well, I am,' Bear repeated.

'I thought it was you making all that thumping noise,' Armadillo went on. 'But it wasn't. It's Elephant. He's teaching himself how to skip.'

'That's good.' Bear was surprised by the change of subject. 'Skipping is good exercise, I suppose, like swimming. Exercise is good for us.'

Armadillo groaned. 'Oh, not you as well. Hare is always going on about exercise, but I would like to ask, what are armchairs for? Sitting in. You may as well not have any armchairs if you're going to exercise all the time.'

Bear didn't know how to answer Armadillo, so he took off his hat and examined it once again. He shuffled a few dead leaves around

with one paw. 'Well, I just thought I'd tell you. Swimming Club starts this afternoon, at the lake. I'm going to tell Jaguar now. If I see Elephant, I'll tell him too.' He ambled off towards the Big Forest.

Hare watched him go. 'I do think Bear is wonderful,' he said.

'Oh, bears,' muttered Armadillo darkly. 'Everybody thinks bears are wonderful. I don't know what others see in them, personally speaking.'

Hare was surprised but decided it was best to leave the matter for the time being. Armadillo was in a grumpy mood, and Hare didn't know why.

Armadillo knew why he was in a grumpy mood, and he didn't like it at all. He had to

admit to himself that he was envious. Bear was popular, especially with Hare.

The Swimming Club was not a success. It was all rather damp. Lobster could already swim, of course. She spent much of the time telling Bear different ways of swimming that she thought were much better.

'I do spend most of my time underwater, after all,' she said crisply. 'In the sea. The sea is much bigger than a lake.'

'Maybe you should spend ALL your time underwater,' Bear growled before adding that swimming was swimming no matter where it was done: the sea, the lake . . . the bath.

Lobster clacked her pincers sharply. She was not at all impressed.

Tortoise found swimming very hard indeed. His body simply wasn't adapted for it. He was not a turtle. He was a tortoise. He sank and had to be rescued several times by Bear, who eventually gave up.

Mouse said she had difficulty walking, let alone swimming and besides, she didn't like waves.

Invisible Stick Insect wouldn't even go near the water. 'I haven't got a swimming costume,' she said coyly.

'But nobody can see you anyway,' Bear pointed out in exasperation. All the animals were being awkward. Giraffe didn't need to bother. He could wade in until the water was so deep it came up to his chin. He didn't need

to actually swim. Elephant was very good at swimming but was happier rolling about in the muddy shallows and singing.

'Phoowee! This is fun!'

Hare splashed about furiously. He was determined to swim but kept disappearing downwards. He would surface, spluttering and feeling very ungainly and inelegant. His ears quickly became quite waterlogged, and he soon gave up altogether.

The biggest surprise was Armadillo. He swam beautifully, effortlessly, gracefully. When he finally came back to shore everyone clapped and cheered, especially Hare.

'I had no idea you were so brilliant!' Hare told his friend. 'I'm astonished! I do so wish I could swim like you.'

Armadillo's heart swelled with pride. 'Thank you Hare. Of course, my father was a swimming champion. He taught me the 'Dillo Dash. It's like Doggy-Paddle but more, um, Armadillo-ish.'

All of them were tired after their exercise. Giraffe and Elephant fell asleep on the bank. Tortoise and Hare sat together. They helped each other by agreeing that they didn't really want to swim anyway. There were better things to do.

'After all, I can run faster than anyone,' Hare told Tortoise.

'And I can run slower than anyone,' Tortoise answered.

But Bear sat all by himself, hunched over and looking like a fallen boulder. Armadillo

went over and sat next to him.

'You were good,' said Bear quietly, without even glancing at Armadillo.

'Thank you.'

'I thought you'd drown, being your shape,' Bear grunted. 'But you swam like a fish.'

For a while, the two animals looked out across the lake. Bear curled his toes a few times and dug them into the earth. He took a deep breath.

'Sometimes,' he confessed in a small voice, 'I feel like I'm a nobody.'

Silence. Armadillo thought carefully. This was a new situation for them both. 'Nobody's a nobody,' he said. 'If you see what I mean.'

'I am. I thought having a swimming club would help, but it hasn't.' Bear paused before going on. 'You see, when I'm on stage with my drums, I forget I'm a nobody. I make a lot of noise, and for a while I feel like I'm somebody. And when I'm almost a doctor, with my box of bandages, I'm needed.'

Bear heaved a long sigh. He dug his toes

even further into the mud beside the lake. 'But deep down inside, I know I'm still a nobody.'

Armadillo considered this for a while. It all seemed too sad. Poor Bear! He wasn't a noisy show off after all. He just wanted to be – someone. The drumming, the hat, Hare's scarves, Elephant's skipping, even Armadillo's slippers! Those things made a someone not a nobody.

Armadillo sighed. Bear needed cheering up, and Armadillo knew just how to do that. He put an arm round Bear's big shoulders.

'I don't suppose you'd like a cheese sandwich?' he suggested. 'I've got some in the fridge at home that we could share.'

Bear turned his big head towards Armadillo and nodded. 'I do like cheese,' he admitted.

Armadillo beamed back. 'The cheese is this way,' he said.

Because It's There

Armadillo was standing on the front porch of the little cabin. Breakfast was finished, and now he was gazing at the Big Forest, which stretched all the way along the far edge of the meadow. The forest looked dark, deep and mysterious.

'What are you doing, Armadillo? You've been out here for ages.' Hare was wearing his favourite green jacket and a new lemon-coloured silk scarf casually draped in a long loop over both shoulders. He was holding two cups of coffee. He handed one to his companion.

'I've been looking at the Big Forest,' said Armadillo. 'I have realised that even forests have moods. Look at it now. It's in a thoughtful, brooding mood.'

Hare brightened. 'Ah! That's *your* mood, Armadillo. You're putting your own mood on the forest. I've read about that sort of thing in one of my books. It was about how we think.'

Armadillo was amused by this. 'Really? Do you know what I'm thinking then, Hare? Can you read my thoughts?'

Hare shook his head. 'Of course I don't know what you are thinking. I simply meant . . .' Hare broke off for a moment. 'Actually, I'm not sure what I meant,' he added with a weak smile.

Armadillo patted Hare's shoulder. 'It doesn't matter. I shall tell you what I was thinking. It occurred to me that the Big Forest we can see at this moment is like a wardrobe.'

Hare spluttered into his coffee. 'What?'

'I said, the Big Forest today is like a wardrobe.' Armadillo had a twinkle in his eye. 'It has closed itself. The door is shut and we can't see inside. Inside is a mystery.'

Hare stared at the forest, the dark trees and bushes, the endless shadows. No matter how long he looked, the forest remained closed to him, like a wardrobe with a shut door, he supposed.

'So, the Big Forest has different moods,' Armadillo continued. 'Remember how sunny it was yesterday? The forest looked different then. It seemed . . .' Armadillo thought for a few seconds, 'almost playful. But now, autumn is coming. The forest is getting ready for winter. So should we. We shall have to bring in wood for the fire.'

The two of them stayed on the porch, finishing their coffee. They watched the passing shadows from the clouds as they shifted across the meadow and the forest beyond.

Hare slowly smoothed one long ear. 'I think you're a bit of a poet, my friend.'

Armadillo chuckled. 'A bit of a poet, eh? Which bit would that be, Hare? My toe? Do I have a poet's toe? A poet's snout? Which bit?'

'You know perfectly well what I mean,' Hare answered evenly.

Hare would have said more, but at that moment they heard a 'ping-ping' and a 'parp-parp' and Wombat came into view. The acrobatic creature was riding her bicycle backwards. This is a difficult trick because if

you are facing backwards you can't see where you are going. It also means sitting on the handlebars. It requires back to front thinking.

It was a new trick for Wombat, and Armadillo and Hare could see that she was having problems. Luckily, Lobster was riding in the little basket that hung from the handlebars, and she was giving Wombat noisy advice. 'Go left! Left! No, LEFT!'

It didn't make any difference because although Lobster was at the front she was behind Wombat, so Wombat couldn't see any of Lobster's frantic pointing. Armadillo shouted a warning but it was too late. Wombat managed to cycle straight into Armadillo and Hare's front porch.

For a moment, the bicycle stayed upright

before finally toppling over, taking Wombat
and Lobster with it.

Lobster crawled out of the basket and
looked accusingly at Wombat. 'I said left.'

'I need more practice,' puffed Wombat.

'Good morning,' Armadillo began dryly. 'Were you planning to ride into our breakfast?'

'Actually, we are going on an exploration.' Lobster spoke crisply. 'Like explorers.'

Armadillo grunted. 'I've never heard of explorers riding bicycles backwards. Have you, Hare?'

Hare shook his head, and Wombat laughed. 'I just need more practice,' she repeated. 'Anyhow, I'm taking Lobster to see the other side of the Big Forest. She's never been there.'

Armadillo frowned. 'What's wrong with here?'

'Because it's not there, of course,' said Hare. He understood at once.

Armadillo's eyes widened in surprise. 'Hare,

sometimes you say the most extraordinary things. Of course here isn't there. If it was there it wouldn't be here, would it?'

Wombat waved her pretty paws in the air. 'That's not what Hare meant at all. What he meant was Here can't be like There. The whole point of There is that There is somewhere else, and new.'

'Yes,' snapped Lobster, folding her claws across her chest. 'And that's where we're going.'

Armadillo shook his head. Here, there, it was all the same to him as long as he was at home. 'Well, stay safe,' he said.

'And watch out for Jaguar,' added Hare.

'Jaguar?' Lobster scoffed. 'She doesn't bother me. If she comes too close I shall box her ears.' Lobster unfolded her snappers and began shadow boxing, landing punches in the air on her invisible opponent.

'You're very brave,' Hare told Lobster as she climbed back into the bicycle's basket.

Lobster stiffened her shoulders. 'I'm not scared of anyone. Come on, Wombat.'

Armadillo cleared his throat loudly. 'If you're going off adventuring on that noisy bicycle of yours, it might be a good idea to face the right way, this time, Wombat,' he advised.

Wombat gave an embarrassed laugh and sat on the saddle properly. Hare waved goodbye.

Wombat pinged the bell, and Lobster parped
the bicycle's horn.

Soon, Armadillo and Hare disappeared
from sight as the two adventurers reached the
edge of the forest. The trees and the shadows
and the silence closed around them.

The forest was darker than Lobster had
imagined. There was a sudden movement

amongst the trees. Could that have been Jaguar with her sharp teeth?

'What was that?'

'Probably a bird,' suggested Wombat.

'Don't you know? It might be something dangerous.'

'I don't think there are any dangerous birds in the Big Forest.'

'Is it far to the other side?' was Lobster's next question.

'I've never been there myself. Hare told me about the rabbit clearing, but he was mostly walking. He only ran a bit,' Wombat added, steadily pedalling.

'Why was Hare running? Was he being chased?'

'He didn't say,' Wombat replied. Lobster

sank into silence, thinking about all the things that might have been chasing Hare. She wished her heart wasn't beating quite so noisily.

By the time they reached the other side of the Big Forest, Lobster was feeling rather unsettled. They came out of the trees at last. There was the sun, a cool blue sky and . . . Elephant.

'Phoowee! What are you two doing here?' exclaimed Elephant. 'You're a long way from home.'

'We're exploring. We've been – in there!' Lobster exclaimed excitedly. She pointed back at the Big Forest.

Elephant nodded. He spent a lot of his time 'in there' so he didn't share Lobster's sense of achievement. 'And now you're out here,' he observed, curling his trunk up to scratch one very large ear. 'What do you think?'

'I think—' Lobster broke off and suddenly scurried backwards. 'What's that?' she demanded.

'What's what?' asked Wombat and Elephant together.

'That! That wriggly thing.'

Elephant and Wombat scanned the ground but could see nothing.

'THAT WRIGGLY THING THERE!'

Elephant and Wombat looked more closely. 'Oh, that,' said Elephant. 'Sheesh! I thought you'd seen a monster. That's Centipede.'

Lobster's giant claws were trembling. 'It's got far too many legs and it wriggles and it's . . . COMING MY WAY! Come-on-Wombat-we-have-to-go-now-we've-seen-the-other-side-we're-going-Elephant-nice-to-see-you-good-bye.'

By this time Lobster was firmly back in the bicycle basket. Elephant watched with mild surprise as Wombat parped and pinged, and the pair set off back through the Big Forest. It took a while for Lobster's frantic heartbeat to settle, but by the time they were halfway home, she found the darkness and the silence of the forest a comfort. She even fell asleep and didn't wake until she heard voices. She opened her eyes to find that they had reached the log cabin in the meadow and Armadillo was peering into the bicycle's basket.

'You're back,' said Armadillo. 'How was your exploring?'

'We saw a monster with far too many legs,' Lobster answered.

'Giraffe?' Armadillo suggested. 'I always think he's got too many legs.'

Lobster was indignant. 'Not Giraffe. I have danced with Giraffe and he is a gentleman.'

'Lobster saw Centipede,' Wombat explained quietly, with a quick wink.

'Oh, Centipede!' Armadillo's eyebrows shot up his head. 'Well, Lobster, here's an interesting thing. When you meet a monster, if you say to them "Hello" and "How are you?" it often turns out that they're not monsters at all. In fact, it's possible they might be just as scared of you. Anyhow, you both look exhausted. Why don't you come inside for some tea and cheesecake before you both go home to bed?'

As they went into the cabin, Hare prodded Armadillo. 'I knew you were going to say that bit about tea and cheesecake,' he said, proudly. 'I read your thoughts.'

'Well, I bet you don't know what I'm thinking now,' Armadillo began. Hare shook his head. 'I'm thinking of giving all your cake to Mouse!' Armadillo started to laugh. 'So there!'

But of course Armadillo did no such thing.

Nothing Really

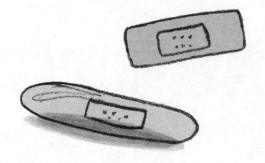

The rain had stopped at last, and the sun appeared to be in a slow waltz with the remaining grey clouds. Hare opened the front door. He went onto the porch and held out a paw. Not a drop. Satisfied, he went back indoors.

'We've been stuck inside for hours,' he told Armadillo. 'We should go out for some fresh air and exercise.'

Armadillo put down the magazine he had been reading. (It was *Sudoku for Armadillos*.) He looked at his friend with deep despair. 'Exercise? Why? You're always exercising,

Hare. Is it not possible to simply sit in an armchair and be still for a while?'

'We have been still all morning,' Hare pointed out irritably. 'You will probably die in that armchair if you stay there any longer. I'm going to drag you outside if it kills me!'

'If you drag me outside I shall probably kill you myself!' Armadillo shot back. For a moment they glared at each other, then burst into laughter.

'All right,' sighed Armadillo. 'We shall go for a walk. I suppose it is rather stuffy indoors. We could visit Giraffe. I do find his legs fascinating. And he always makes me think I'm talking to royalty. I suppose it's because everyone looks up to him.'

'You *have* to look up to him,' Hare said

pointedly. 'He's taller than anyone else. I shall wear my new jacket in case it rains again.'

Armadillo pulled on his old coat, the one with a torn sleeve and two missing buttons. Hare slipped on a jazzy bright-yellow rain jacket. It had a hood that folded into the collar and a special hidden pocket.

'I hope nobody sees us,' muttered Armadillo, casting a glance at Hare's bright jacket. 'They'll think I'm taking a large daffodil for a walk.'

'That's not funny,' Hare said, a trifle stiffly.

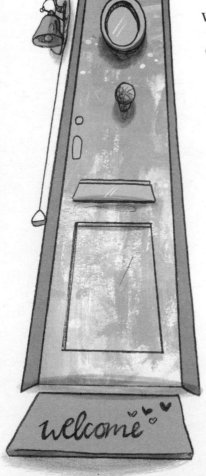

The pair set off. The sun was still dancing with the clouds. One moment the grass would be glinting with tiny lights and then a cloud shadow would snuff them out, only for the sun to appear elsewhere.

Giraffe lived at the end of the Big Forest. However, he didn't seem to be at home that morning.

104

'He might have gone to see someone himself,' suggested Hare.

Armadillo considered this. 'You could be right. But suppose Giraffe has gone to see Tortoise, and he finds that Tortoise isn't there because Tortoise has gone to see Wombat. But when Tortoise gets to Wombat's place, Wombat isn't there because Wombat has gone to see Elephant. And when Wombat gets to—'

'I get the picture,' Hare hastily interrupted. His ears had gone quite out of control and were jerking about.

Armadillo shrugged. 'Oh well, I suppose we may as well walk back. Perhaps we shall see him on the way.'

They had barely taken three steps when they heard a rustling and a deep sigh behind them. They turned, and there was Giraffe, stepping out from between the trees.

'Giraffe!' Armadillo cried. 'What's happened? You're limping. Are you hurt?'

'Oh, it's nothing really,' droned Giraffe. 'Just a bit of knee trouble. Ignore it. I expect it will go away.'

The lofty creature stopped to lean against a tree and rest his injured leg. 'Ow,' he murmured. 'So tell me, how are you both keeping? That's a very smart coat you have, Hare. Are you worried you might get lost?'

Hare's ears did a bit more frantic jerking. 'Sorry? I don't understand.'

Giraffe gave a slow smile. 'I thought perhaps if you got lost then we would be able to find you quickly. Your coat is quite, erm, noticeable.'

Hare blushed. His ears began to droop.

Armadillo thought of several jokes of his own he might add about the yellow jacket, but he kept quiet. Hare was embarrassed enough already. In any case, it was clear that Giraffe's leg was giving him a lot of trouble.

'Can you sit?' Armadillo asked.

Giraffe sighed. 'I can, but it's not a natural position for someone at my level, so to speak. It's a long way down and rather uncomfortable.'

'Even so, you should rest that leg,' said Armadillo. 'We need to get you some help.'

'Oh, it's nothing really,' Giraffe repeated. 'I do hate it when a fuss is made.'

'I can understand that,' said Armadillo. 'I'm the same.'

Hare shot a surprised look at his friend.

'You! You make a fuss over nothing. What about this morning when you couldn't find your toothbrush?'

Armadillo tried to change the subject. 'This isn't about me, Hare. We need to help Giraffe. How are we going to do that?'

Hare brightened and his ears pinged upright. 'Bear! He's been to first-aid classes. He's a doctor, well, almost. I'll go and find him.'

Hare set off at once leaving Armadillo to keep Giraffe company. Armadillo began by asking how had Giraffe hurt his knee.

'I was doing my morning yoga exercises,' Giraffe intoned. 'My foot

slipped on the wet grass. I managed to stay upright, but I twisted my knee.'

'It does look rather swollen.' Armadillo nodded. 'That's the problem with exercises. You can end up worse than when you started, and for that reason, I avoid them.'

By the time Hare returned with Bear, word had got around about Giraffe's misfortune. A small group of animals had gathered.

Bear brought with him his white box with a red cross on it. Now he examined the swollen knee. 'Is it sore?' he asked.

'Oh, it's nothing really,'

sighed Giraffe for the third time.

'If I poke it gently, does it hurt?' asked Bear.

'Ow. No, it doesn't hurt, not really. I can manage,' said Giraffe bravely.

Bear gave his patient a stern look. 'Giraffe, you have a badly twisted knee and I know that it is giving you a lot of pain. You are going to have to stay still so I can treat you. I can bandage your knee in such a way that you will be able to stand again. Now then, what we need for this swollen knee is an ice pack. Does anyone have an ice pack?'

Bear looked around at the assembled animals. They shook their heads, all of them except for Armadillo.

'I don't exactly have an ice pack,' he began. 'But I do have a bag of grated cheese in the freezer. Would that help?'

Bear lifted his big head and smiled at

Armadillo. 'You, my friend, are a hero. A packet of frozen grated cheese would be perfect.'

'It's Parmesan,' Armadillo added proudly, turning to the others. 'Excellent for special occasions,' he told them. 'Such as spaghetti, or risotto.'

'This is a special occasion,' Bear pointed out.

'Hmmm,' grunted Armadillo. Giraffe's knee was not the sort of special Parmesan occasion Armadillo had in mind. Hare squeezed his friend's paw. He understood what a sacrifice Armadillo was making.

'I'll run back and get it,' said Hare, and off he went for the second time.

While Hare was collecting the grated cheese, the other animals wondered how they could help Giraffe.

'I'm quite all right,' said Giraffe, settling back. 'It's nothing really. Ow.'

Hare returned, having raced to the log cabin and back. He was panting. He pulled his jacket back into shape and handed the little frozen packet of grated cheese to Bear.

Bear knew what he was doing. He really had been to first-aid classes. He carefully placed the cold bag over Giraffe's swollen knee. He wrapped padding over the top and then wound a long bandage round and round so that the knee was supported tightly.

'Try standing up,' Bear told his patient.

Giraffe slowly got back to his feet and tested

his injured leg. 'Oh,' he said. 'That's much better. My goodness, Bear, you have hidden talents. I bow before you.' Giraffe swept his head low across Bear's feet.

The animals patted each other on the back. Some shouted 'Hooray for Bear!' Invisible Stick Insect even shouted 'Happy Birthday, Giraffe!' having got rather over-excited. After that, there was nothing more to see and they began to drift away.

Armadillo and Hare set off for home.

When they reached the cabin, Hare sat on the porch and started blowing into his tuba. Out came an assortment of bandages, scissors, toilet roll and a hospital bed.

Armadillo watched them fade away. 'It's a strange thing you know,' he mused. 'Fancy Bear knowing first aid. You can be friends with someone, but I don't think you can ever know everything about them. There'll always be surprises. Yes, indeed.' He licked his lips. 'I think I'm going to make myself a cheese sandwich now.'

'That's not a surprise,' said Hare. He turned to the fridge. 'You must remember to put Parmesan on the shopping list!'

Watching the Moon

'You're always reading,' Armadillo told Hare one morning. 'Look at you, nose stuck in a book.'

'My nose isn't stuck to anything,' Hare replied evenly. 'And this is a newspaper.'

'Well, in that case, don't do the sudoku puzzle. I like doing that. It's supposed to be good exercise for the brain, which is the kind of exercising I like,' Armadillo shot back. 'No jogging or press-ups for me. Look what happened to Giraffe when he did his yoga!'

'Have you finished?' asked Hare with amusement, peering at Armadillo over the top of his spectacles.

'Yes!' snapped Armadillo. He rubbed his snout quickly to hide his own smile.

Hare held up the newspaper. 'It says here that there will be a full moon tonight, a special one, bigger than usual.'

'Really? I didn't know the moon could change size.'

'Of course it can't,' Hare told him. 'But sometimes it comes closer to Earth, and then it looks bigger.'

'Is that so? Well, I think you look bigger when you're further away, but when you get close to me I suddenly realise that you're quite titchy really.' Armadillo gave a loud snort and couldn't stop his shoulders heaving with chuckles.

'You're in one of your silly moods,' Hare observed. 'I shall ignore you. Anyhow, you will like the next bit. Apparently the moon will rise over the Big Forest just after dark.' Hare began to read from the newspaper. '*When the moon appears it will be larger than normal and yellow in colour. Astronomers have named tonight's rising moon the "Big Cheese Moon".*'

Armadillo sat up straight, speechless for a moment: 'The Big Cheese Moon?'

Hare nodded and held out the newspaper so Armadillo could read the article for himself.

'The Big Cheese Moon,' repeated Armadillo when he had finished. 'You know what this means, Hare, don't you? We must celebrate. We must gather on the meadow after dark so we can all watch the Big Cheese Moon rise. This is wonderful! I shall go and see Wombat. She can get round to all the others on her bicycle and tell them about tonight. This is something we must not miss!'

Armadillo was almost trembling in his red slippers. 'Hare! I am so excited!'

Hare chuckled. 'I can see. Well, if we are going to have a party tonight there is lots to do. We shall need chairs, tables, food and entertainment. We had better get to work.'

With Wombat's help, the news spread rapidly amongst the animals. Even the few clouds that were slowly passing overhead seemed to be excited. At least Armadillo thought so.

Giraffe was very happy to learn that there would be dancing. His knee had improved rapidly, thanks to Armadillo's emergency frozen cheese. Giraffe loved to dance, but very few of the animals knew that he also liked to sing.

'I shall sing with the band. It's nothing really, just a little something I do sometimes,'

Giraffe declared from on high. 'And since it is such a special occasion I shall bring my chandelier.'

An excited murmur went round the Big Forest. 'Giraffe is bringing his chandelier. No, I don't know what it is either, but Giraffe is bringing it.'

Lobster was not impressed by cheese moons or chandeliers, but said she would come because it meant she could dance with Giraffe.

'I think you have fallen in love with him,' teased Tortoise.

Lobster turned bright red and clacked her pincers angrily. 'Don't be ridiculous, Tortoise.' She turned her back on him and marched off.

'Lobster is *en amour*,' said Tortoise (who had a French mother, Madame Tortue). 'She is in *lurve*,' he added with a wink.

By the end of the afternoon, everything was ready. A line of chairs, none of them matching, stood in the meadow facing the Big Forest. There was no chair for Elephant or Giraffe, but Armadillo had thoughtfully provided two large rugs and some soft cushions.

As the sun sank lower, Jaguar strolled out from the Big Forest. When she saw all the others sitting in a line and staring back at her (some with alarm) she stopped and gave a little curtsy.

'Good evening everyone,' she purred in a low voice. 'Settle down now, I'm not going to eat any of you – today.' Was Jaguar joking, the animals wondered? Probably. But of course for most small animals, 'probably' never feels safe enough.

Hare shuffled nearer to Armadillo.

'If you get any closer you'll be hiding under my cardigan with Mouse. But I'm sure there's room for the three of us.'

The sun dipped slowly to the horizon. The sky turned pink, then red, then purple, then

silky black. Out came the stars, cascading into the sky in their millions. Their glitter was matched on the meadow by the glinting of Jaguar's huge sharp eyes in the dark.

A shooting star briefly burned a sparkling

track across the heavens. Those who glimpsed it widened their eyes and went 'Ahh!'

'We don't need fireworks tonight,' Tortoise observed.

Lobster folded her claws across her chest. 'I think fireworks are—'

But the animals never heard what Lobster thought fireworks were because out of the forest stepped the most extraordinary sight. It was Giraffe, and it seemed as if his head was ablaze with light.

Every candle on Giraffe's chandelier was lit and he was wearing it like a hat. The little flames reflected and sparkled in each teardrop crystal hanging from the branches of the chandelier. It tinkled as he strode towards them.

'It looks as if he's grown flaming horns!' cried Wombat with delight.

'Stunning,' murmured Bear.

'The moon! Look at the moon!' shouted Hare.

First there was a small sliver of cheese above

the Big Forest. The sliver became a wedge and then bit by bit all was revealed. For a moment the cheese moon seemed to be caught by the topmost branches of the Big Forest, but then they let go. It sailed clear. Astonishing. Rapturous. Beautiful beyond words.

Armadillo felt as if he had been transported to heaven. The moon was so very huge, so very golden and so very magnificent.

'It really does look as if it is made of cheese,' he said, with enormous satisfaction.

Hare nodded. 'Though even you couldn't eat a cheese that big,' he pointed out. 'I think it's time for the band to play.' And play they did.

Bear banged his drums. Hare puffed into his tuba and Invisible Stick Insect was very busy on the triangle. As Hare blew into his tuba, out came masses of miniature stars and planets and moons, little rockets, several space buggies and a telescope.

Giraffe sang, as he had promised. It was singing that no animal had ever heard

before. The audience was transfixed. Giraffe's enormous tongue flopped about like some strange creature trying to escape from his mouth. There were no words or tune, simply a long and extraordinary low howling directed at the Big Cheese Moon. It was magical and majestic.

Finally, as the band played their last number, with Bear thrashing the drums into an exciting climax, Wombat appeared on her bicycle. The clever creature had attached a dynamo to one wheel. It provided electricity for the dozens of little coloured lights she had threaded through the spokes of her wheels and along the bicycle's frame. As she pedalled the whole bike glowed with different colours. 'Parp' went the horn. 'Ping'

went the bell. 'Ting-ting' went Invisible Stick Insect on the triangle.

While all this was going on, Elephant trotted off behind a large bush. When he came back he was holding a giant, silver, moon-shaped balloon.

'I found this on the other side of the forest,' he explained. 'It was caught on the branch of a tree. It took me ages to get it down and bring it here safely. Phoowee! I thought it would burst at any moment. It must have been left over from a party somewhere.'

The balloon tugged at its string as it floated above Elephant's head. It certainly looked like another Big Cheese Moon. Armadillo was entranced.

'It's wonderful. May I hold it?'

'Of course. My pleasure,' said Elephant.

So Armadillo took hold of the string, and before anyone could say 'Phoowee!' Armadillo's feet had left the ground and he began to float away.

'Help! Help me!'

'Let go!' snapped Lobster. 'Let go!'

'I'm too high!' Armadillo shouted back as he drifted upwards. The animals raced after him. But it was Giraffe with his great height who saved him. He sprang into the air.

'A pirouette!' cried Lobster in delight. 'Did you see that? Ballet! Giraffe is so wonderful!'

'*Lurve*,' sniggered Tortoise quietly.

Giraffe said nothing because he had his mouth full. He had grabbed Armadillo's

tail and now he brought them both back to earth.

Armadillo let go of the string and the balloon raced up into the sky. Perhaps it wanted to join the real Big Cheese Moon, which now shone down on all of them, serene, silent and glowing.

'You scared me,' Hare told his friend. 'I was worried you might become the first Armadillo on the moon. I thought I was going to lose you. Don't you do anything like that again.'

Armadillo's snout

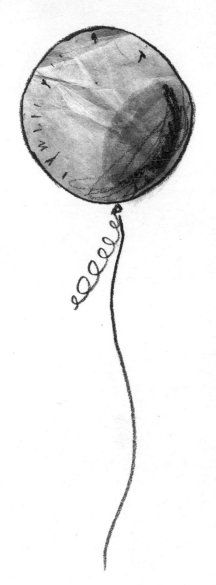

wrinkled into an odd little smile.

'Don't you worry, Hare,' Armadillo answered, as he sat down with a contented sigh. 'I shan't. That was far too much like exercise.'

The party carried on around them. The friends had a real feast, and afterwards Hare played his tuba again. This time tiny sheep came flying softly

out of the instrument. The animals watched,  counted the vanishing sheep, and one by one they fell asleep on the grass.

'This is the best bit with parties,' Armadillo confided in Hare. 'They all go quiet at last. Everyone goes to sleep and they are all happy.'

But Hare was quietly snoring. Armadillo gazed up into the darkness. Above them all several million stars sparkled in the endless black sky and slowly wheeled round as the great Earth turned beneath.

Armadillo and Hare's Short Discussion

It was late evening, and the fire had died away to a few small flames and a lot of glowing embers. Hare had been reading. Armadillo had been travelling in his mind, somewhere between thoughts and dreams. Every so often his head would nod. Now he snorted loudly and lifted his whiskery head with a jerk. 'I think I fell asleep,' he murmured.

'You've been snoring for the last five minutes,' Hare observed. 'Were you dreaming?'

'It was more imagining than dreaming. I was wondering how you came to play the tuba.'

Hare put his book to one side. He pulled at

one long ear, running his paw all the way from the bottom to the top. The ear sprang upright.

'My mother taught me. She was the tuba player in the family, but she got it from her mother, so that would be my grandmother. My grandmother got it from my great great grandmother. My great great grandmother got it from my great great great grandmother. My great great great grandmother got it from my great great—'

'Yes, I get the idea,' Armadillo broke in. 'But who had the tuba at the beginning?'

'Ah, that would be my great great great great great great great – how many is that so far? I've lost track.'

'That's seven greats,' Armadillo chuckled. 'I'm beginning to wish I'd never asked.'

'Altogether there should be nine.' Hare nodded emphatically.

'There's a lot of history in that tuba,' Armadillo said, impressed.

'And there's a lot of history in your red slippers,' Hare pointed out.

'No, just my old feet,' chuckled Armadillo. 'I'll tell you the story of my red slippers another time. Right now what I want to know is how you make all those magical things come out of your tuba.'

Hare had to think hard. He pulled at each ear in turn. He tweaked his whiskers.

'I don't think I "make" them come out. They just do. The way I see it is this – my tuba has been filled with the dreams and feelings of all those who have played it before me. When I play, depending on my mood, it stirs up some of those dreams and feelings and they come drifting out.'

Armadillo considered this for a while, staring into the dying fire. He stretched out his feet so that they were nearer the warmth.

'I think you are right,' Armadillo said. 'But I also think it takes an extraordinary and magical hare to be able to play the tuba so well.' He smiled across at his companion.

'Thank you, Armadillo. But you know, we are all extraordinary in some way or other.'

Armadillo sank further back in his armchair and grunted. 'I'm not so sure.'

'Oh yes,' insisted Hare. 'For example, look at you. Only you can put the buttons in the wrong holes on your cardigan every single day. That is truly extraordinary!'

A cushion came cartwheeling through the air. Hare ducked just in time.

'Time for bed,' laughed Armadillo.

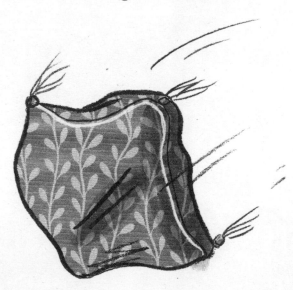